The Dead are
Alive
CHUKWUDI ANYAEGBUNA

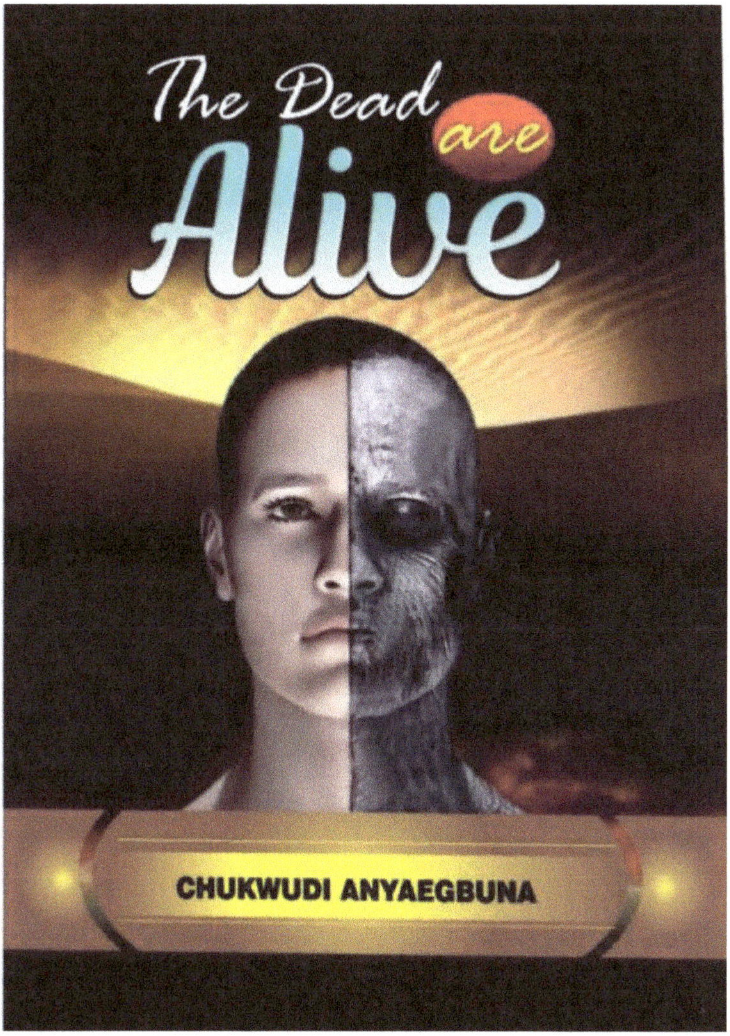

PATRICKCHIDI RIGHT-PATHS LTD

NO 17 OZOMAGALA ROAD

ODOAKPU, ONITSHA

EMAIL: panyaegbuna@gmail.com

To my father, Patrick Francis Ikemefuna Anyaegbuna
who died when I was a kid.

<u>**LOGLINE:**</u>

Clara, a prophetess, unravels the mysteries of the dead: the dead procreate, revenge, avenge, care for the loved ones, and most times need the assistance of the living but difficult to communicate with the living because of the spiritual barriers.

TABLE OF CONTENTS

SYNOPSIS

Clara's father's inordinate quest for riches cost him his family but Clara whose spiritual powers were unparalleled, survived.

She could do what many great men could not do: making the impossibility possible, revealing the hidden messages and bringing solace to many families. Though an ordinary lady, her gifts were too much: seeing, hearing, talking and resuscitating the dead. Healing was part of her endowment.

With her, the mysteries of death were unraveled. She was a go-between between the living and the dead. The dead, especially the good ones, were happy knowing her potentials, for she was the solution to their problems.

Her explorations with the dead, in the anthology of short stories, THE DEAD ARE ALIVE are clear indications that there is life after death and the dead can make love, procreate and fight for their loved ones everywhere.

CHAPTER ONE
I CAN NOW REST

He stood by the side and watched over a woman with a twelve-year-old boy seated on a bench by the roadside. His gaze focused on her sun-flecked face. There was perspiration on her face and dripping sweat on her cheeks. Intermittently, she wiped her face with her tied wrapper. Her light skin was pale having been exposed to lots of sunlight. The wrapper and a gown she was wearing had experienced a lot of water and soap. She looked gaunt in those wears. Her hair was unkempt. The sight of her appearance irked him.

His eyes averted from her and focused on the edibles in her front. They were peppers, sprawled in groups, and at the side of the bench lay a basket of peppers. They were yellow in colour. She was only person having the specie, her neighbours had red-coloured peppers.

From time to time, she stood up and attended to people who wanted to purchase some peppers. Her hands were covered with a hand glove. She put the displayed ones for the buyers and dipped her hands into the basket and replaced them.

"My sweetheart, my sweetheart, please listen." The man said but the unseeing eyes and deaf ears could not see or hear him.

"Who is your sweetheart?" Asked a lady waiting for her turn to purchase the pepper.

"Can you see me?"

"What do you mean by that?"

"Please, don't be afraid. I'm dead."

"You are what?" She impulsively stepped backward and went by the side so that people might not think she was insane.

"Please, I'm sorry but I need your assistance." He followed her.

"You people should leave me alone. I have stopped greeting strangers because of you people."

"After today, I won't disturb you again."

"Alright, what can I do for you?"

"I am Charles. This woman selling pepper is my wife. Her name is Jane. The boy with her is our son, Charles. I died two weeks after his birth. For twelve good years, I have been following them, speaking to them but they could not hear or see me. I thank God you can hear and see me. Please, I have an important message for her. She should not be suffering. Please call her, let me speak to her through you."

"You know you cannot enter into me."

"I don't have permission. You cannot be my medium. I just want you to be a go-between"

"Alright," she said, moving straight to Jane.

"Madam, somebody wants to talk to you."

"Wait. I'm busy, I shall speak to you later."

"Tell Charles to attend to your customers. It's urgent."

"You know my son?"

"Are you not Jane?"

"You know me too."

"Your husband is dead. He died twelve years ago."

"That is correct but who are you?"

"I am Clara. Your husband wants to speak to you."

"How? He is dead."

"But alive only that you can't see him or touch him. He is here."

"Where?"

"Beside you and he loves you so much."

"How I wish I can see him."

"He has a very important message for you."

Before his death, Charles had a series of nightmares where his siblings had the plot to kill him. His town custom and tradition concerning the inheritance of a deceased husband's property were repugnant to natural Justice, equity, and good conscience. He pitied his wife, if peradventure, he was no more. On that strength, he started selling his properties, withdrawing his money from banks, and stalling them away. Unfortunately, his siblings called him on Saturday and notified him of an urgent meeting on Sunday in their town. Charles did not want to go but his wife persuaded him to. He obeyed. On his way back from the meeting Charles had a gruesome accident that claimed his life.

Aware of his death, his siblings came to his place and started looking for documents and passbooks. They were disappointed to find that Charles had nothing. Enmity and regrets struck them. After the burial, Jane started selling peppers.

"Tell her to go to our bed, that ten Million is inside the bed." Clara related the message to Jane who dashed away like a lightning and soon came back confirming the message.

"Tell her to stop selling pepper, rather buy a small land built a bungalow, a shop, she would use as supermarket." Clara did as he said.

"I can now rest." Exhilarated, he raised his hands, wanting to embrace her.

"He is in your front wanting to embrace you" Clara said while Jane embraced the air hilariously.

"How can I repay you?" The husband and wife said simultaneously.

"Don't bother." Replied Clara.

"Can I have your phone number?"

"Don't bother about my phone number. Use the money wisely. You will later see me, I promise."

"At least, accept some peppers from me."

"Please, accept the peppers." Charles pleaded as well as people around.

"Thank you so much, my dear. God shall continue blessing you." Said Jane.

"Amen." Accepting the water proof of peppers from Jane."

"I can now rest. Bid her goodbye for me." Clara related the message to Jane who reciprocated. Then he left, and so did Clara.

CHAPTER TWO
HIS WISH BEFORE DEATH

Her phone buzzed. She picked it.

"Hello, may I know who is calling?"

"Clara, have you forgotten me?"

"Sorry, I lost my phone, please who am I speaking with?"

"Clara, can't you recognize my voice?"

"The voice sounds familiar but I can't place it."

"Guess.'

"I don't have that time."

"Clara, you will never change."

"I have no time for frivolities. I love getting into business."

"There were two virgins in the Daily Star female football team, others are lesbians. One is Clara and the other..."

"Philomena, you should carry your time." Hysteria laughter sounded on the two phones.

"Men are heart breakers are still unmarried?"

"They are making it big in football but they don't know the taste of a gentle husband."

"I know you detest them. If not for you I would have joined them."

"It is a sin against nature, the holy spirit."

"That's by the way. Somebody said something to me and I could not understand it."

"What is that?"

"She said that she would take away my pride and joy."

"Phil, do you have children?"

"No. Have you forgotten that we married early this year and my husband traveled after the marriage?"

"That's true, but are you pregnant?"

"Not at all."

"Your pride and joy is your husband and the person wants to kill him."

"Is not possible, I can't believe you."

"Why?"

"The maker of the statement is my husband's eldest sister, Cecilia. Although she was forcing her partner on my husband, my husband's love for me is everlasting. We are like Siamese that can never be severed. She has made efforts to separate us but all her efforts proved abortive. Her female lover had no option but to marry a man who is based abroad. The man has taken his wife to Canada."

"This is more reason you will believe me. You broke her relationship and you want to enjoy yours. It is not possible."

"My husband is the only male issue they have in their family. She will rather come for my life than kill her only brother."

"Jealousy, grievance, and hatred have beclouded her sense of reasoning. The power of virginity before marriage is your strength against her"

"I don't believe you. How can a woman kill her only brother? Her father's household shall become extinct. I don't believe you."

"Believe it or not, start praying for your joy so that nothing will happen to him."

"I don't believe you." The phone went off and Phil went to the Parlour.

She paced her parlour to and fro wondering how possible what Clara told her was. Her husband had called some minutes ago that he would be at home in less than thirty minutes and she was waiting happily for his arrival when her sister-in-law vomited the garbage. At a time, she lay on a couch but was restless. She scrambled to her feet wanted to soothe her feelings with music but there was no electricity supply. She remembered her cell phone. It was not in the parlour but in the bedroom, she thought.

Inside the bedroom, she beheld the phone on the bed. Picking it up, her fingers mistakenly struck a number while she was scrolling for music. He looked at the name. It was coach Sam.

Coach Sam was their coach on the Daily Star Female football team. He was her husband's uncle and was the person that linked her to her husband. His joy was seeing her together with her husband. It was his effort that shattered Cecilia's plan of keeping her lover in the family.

"Hello, Phil. How are you?" Coach Sam's voice sounded.

"I am restless."

"Why?"

"Cecilia said that she would take away my pride and joy. I called Clara, she told me my pride and joy is my husband."

"Cecilia is hard-hearted but I don't think she can kill her only brother."

"I think so and I told Clara it is not possible."

"Is she the Clara that played 9 in our team?"

"Yes."

"She possesses some spiritual powers and you shouldn't dismiss her advice with a wave of the hand. But I still have reservations about how Cecilia can think of killing her only brother." There was a bang at the door and clatter in the parlour.

"I shall call you later." She said, cutting the call and leaving the cell phone on the bed. Entering the parlour, she saw her husband's picture formerly on the wall now on floor, shattered. She was surprised as her eyes beheld her husband seated on the sofa with his both palms on his cheeks and tears twinkling down his cheeks.

"What is the problem and when did you come in?"

"I came in when you were on calls. When I remembered the accident on the road, I could not withhold my tears."

"I thank God you are at home. I was afraid of what Cecilia said"

"I don't want to hear that name. She is foolish and must face the law of Karma."

"Once more, I thank God you are back."

"But I shall go out now to come back later. I am hungry."

"I prepared a delicious meal for you."

"You are the delicacies I need. I am hungry for you."

"I am all yours. Do with me what thy will." He smothered her with kisses as both of them put themselves in the purest state of nature just before

Adam and Eve ate the forbidden fruit. His sensual caresses sent a sensual sensation like electric vibes through her body. She encircled her hands tightly on her neck, pushing her entire body so tight to his. Each of them wanted to consume the other. He carried her as a mother cuddled her baby, took her into the bedroom, and lay her gently there. Her finger got hold of the real man while his hands sought for the holy of holies, the source of all mankind. Both attended to the two most important parts of the body until they were ready for the fulfillment of God's injunction. The two met at the confluence, overflowing each other, sending sensations to each other with the lady producing reflex sounds and the man doing continuous press up until the two reached the climax and their energies dwindled.

"Since we married, this is the best so far." She said.

"How I wish I could give it to you again but I am happy my seeds are there"

"What do you mean?"

"You are pregnant with twins, a boy and a girl."

"You are joking. Even the scan cannot know whether I am pregnant at this stage. It is only the Prophet that can know."

"I am more than a prophet." He got up, went to the parlour, dressed up, and sat on the sofa. He scribbled something on a paper with the pen he took from the centre table. He gave it to her with his ATM card.

"This is your password."

"Yes, it is my pin number. Commit it to memory and destroy it at once. He went inside and came out with his briefcase and handed some documents to her.

"These are the documents to my landed property, keep it at the bottom of your clothes' box. Let nobody know about the ATM and the documents. After the raining they shall be useful to you?"

"It is not raining."

"Remember that six months shall pass before you see me again. Let nobody pressurize you into searching for me before the six months. Within those six months and after, never have any regrets. Only make sure you say your prayers, do your responsibility and enjoy, for this life has no duplicate."

"I am confused, my dear. You are getting me worried."

"Don't be worried. I'll always be with you and fight for you. It's time for me to leave." She dressed up and saw him off. He kissed her on the cheeks, forehead, and stomach and bade her goodbye. Taking two steps forward, he looked back and their eyes met. He came back, embracing her and saying. "Be strong. I am with you always."

She stared at him until he evaporated into thin air. She then got into their room and heard her phone. Before she could pick it up, it was off. She looked at it, eight missed calls: six from the same caller and two from the coach. She decided to return the call of the highest caller and her phone started ringing again.

"Are you the wife of Anthony." A male voice asked.

"Yes, I am." She replied.

"Your husband had an accident thirty minutes ago."

"That's not my husband."

"I shall call you with his number. It has a low battery." As the phone went off, coach Sam called and she picked the call.

"Hello, Phil, where are you?"

"My house."

"I'm coming."

After ten minutes, her husband phone number called.

"Hello, sweetheart." She said.

"I'm doctor Raymond. Are you alone. Your husband had an accident Forty minutes ago."

"It's not possible. I was with my husband Twenty minutes ago and we had good times."

"You mean he had sex with you?"

"Yes, as we have never done before. Why am telling you all these?"

"So he has fulfilled his wish before death."

"What are you talking about" A knock sounded. She went and opened the door. In front of her, stood coach Sam who entered and sat down.

"Is anybody there with you?"

"Yes, coach Sam is here? I know Coach Sam and I had earlier spoken to her. She will let you know what happened." The phone went off.

"Coach, Dr. Raymond said that you have a message for me."

"Your husband had an accident."

"No coach, it is not possible. My husband left here not too long ago and we had sexual intercourse."

The door opened and Cecilia entered.

"I heard my brother is dead, where is his body."

"Not true, my husband is not dead. He was here not too long ago."

"His death has affected you psychologically."

"His wish according to the doctor was that he would not be buried until after six months."

"That is not possible we shall bury him at once. He has no issue. After the burial, his wife can remarry since my late brother has no issue. Uncle, you should tell me the name of the doctor and the hospital."

"I don't know the name of the hospital. Your brother said that he would be buried after six months. We shall respect his wish."

"I shall investigate and sue that hospital. I shall get an injunction compelling them to release the corpse for burial"

"While are you too serious about the burial? Your brother just died"

"There is nowhere one's relation is dead and the hospital retains his corpse stating that it shall be released after six months. That hospital should tell the court why they are retaining his body. Do they have hands in his death?"

She left in a rage and sought the hospital but could not find it. She brought the case to the town and the hearing was fixed in a fortnight. During the hearing, Coach Sam was asked to invite doctor Raymond. Doctor Raymond came and provided Anthony's phone number which recorded his wish. Doctor Raymond put on Anthony's phone records of his wish. "My wish is to have children. I shall never be buried until after six months so that the person that killed me would not cage my spirit."

 Philemon narrated her experience and a scan was conducted, showing her pregnancy and that she had twins.

"So Tony finally fulfilled HIS WISH BEFORE DEATH by impregnating his wife after he died. This is incredible." Coach Sam said.

CHAPTER THREE
HIS MOTHER'S WISH

She wailed and rolled on the ground, refusing to be consoled. She wanted to jump into a grave when a casket containing her only surviving son was laid into the grave, but consolers intercepted her. She lamented and wanted to curse God but resisted the impulse, instead started eulogizing God, to people's chagrin.

"Since it is your wish that I am an orphan, I glorify your name. Since it's your wish that I am a widow, I glorify your name. Since it's your wish that I am childless, I glorify your name. I am now old. Once I am late, my household and my husband's household are late. You are all-powerful, all-knowing and faithful. I have worshipped you throughout my life, don't forsake me."

After the burial, She stayed in only three places: home, market and the church. At home after her house chores, she visited her son's tomb, asking him to come back to her. In the church, she frequented the grotto of the blessed virgin Mary, saying her rosary and praying that his child would be back. At the market, she no longer discussed with the neighbours. People gossiped that the loss of her only son had left her deranged.

Days turned into weeks, weeks into months, months into years, she maintained her habit until one Evening, she was at her son's grave, calling him to come back when a car drove inside her compound, an elegant fair lady with two boys and two girls alighted from the car.

"Good Evening, ma." they came closer to her.

"Good evening. Who are you looking for?"

"Mrs Mary Okonkwo, my mother-in-law."

"I am Mrs. Mary Okonkwo but you are missing the road."

"No, my husband showed me this place and asked me to drive into the compound that he wanted to see somebody and would be back."

"Who is your husband?"

"Mr. John Okonkwo."

"Madam," Mrs. Mary rose and touched her on the neck, "are you sure you are not suffering from acute malaria."

"Mama, what are all these? What kind of embarrassment is this?"

"Sorry my daughter, what you're saying is impossible. Anyway, do you have any picture of your husband?"

"As if he knew you would doubt us, he gave me his picture." She opened her purse, brought the picture, and handed it over to her.

"It is true, it is true. Neighbours come! The impossible has happened. Neighbours come!! Neighbours comeooo!!!" She dashed out of the compound, her wrapper pulling out and she tied it firmly. John's wife gaped at the old woman. Some villagers started gathering, some who saw her as deranged, pitied her, and ignored her.

"Clara, you told me my son would wipe away my tears; that his father's household would never die, it was hard to believe but I know you are a great prophetess." Mary said as her eyes caught the sight of a lady among the villagers.

"Your son is here. He brought me here to tell you to welcome his wife and your grandchildren and to ask his wife, Lucy, for forgiveness." Clara said while Lucy looked aghast at them.

"Tell him, I have accepted them already."

"He said thank you so much."

"Thank him for me."

"He is happy for you"

"What is happening. How do you know my name?" Lucy asked.

"Your husband told me and he seeks your forgiveness. He is a dead person."

"How do you expect me to believe you? I came to this town with my husband who told me to drive in that he wanted to see a person and he would be here later. Give us a seat, let us wait for him."

"Please, my children, come inside and sit down." Mrs Mary took the lead into the parlour, John's family, Clara and others followed.

"There is no need waiting for your husband to come. You can never see him again physically; you can only see him in your dreams. Your husband knows I see the dead persons and he came to me to help him out "

"How can I be sure? Are you telling me that for the past twelve years, I have been living with a dead man?"

"I have his poster, he pleaded with me to keep it, that there would be a time I would use it. This is the poster." As lucy caught a glimpse of that poster, she fainted and later came to consciousness.

"So all the while, I have been living with a dead person."

"Your husband loves you so much and had wanted he stay with you but you have disturbed her a lot and he doesn't want to see you unhappy so he decided to reveal the secret."

"Was it why for so many years we have lived in Port Harcourt, he didn't want to take us home?"

"That was the reason. He now wants you to forgive him and to take care of his children and mother. He said that if you manage his investments well, you shall never lack."

"Tell him, I have forgiven him and I promise to do his will."

"He is happy and thank you so much. He said that he married you to fulfil his mother's wish and that his mother has challenged the Almighty God to the extent that he was granted permission to do the impossible. He said that he would be leaving but from time to time he shall visit you in your dreams. He also asks you to take his mother to his house at Port Harcourt."

"I shall do that." Lucy said and Clara left.

CHAPTER FOUR
MY SECOND WIFE

She slipped and was fighting not to fall when her money fell into a turbulent flood in a gutter. Her previous views of the gutter revealed that the gully was almost her size. Impulsively she wanted to jump into the gutter but resisted the temptation, apart from the dangers of being drowned, the deluge had driven the money very far from her sight.

Staring at the torrent and thinking about her only means of survival vanishing therein, she wanted to cry but held herself. Tears welled in her eyes and later surged down her cheeks. Her protruded stomach ladened her waste with a kick therein. She trudged and sat on an elevated structure. The palm fronds where she sat under moved to and fro, producing crackling sounds and sending shivers upon her. Droppings fell by her side, as she heard the chirping and fluttering of birds. Looking up, she beheld birds in nuptial flight and wished her husband was at home.

A vroom vroom sound erupted and her eyes riveted towards the direction and caught sight of a very clean motorcycle. Its rider appeared in an immaculate Brazier suit, a mafia one, and a very expensive white pair of shoes. On his neck was a gold chain, glittering. His wristwatch was equally gold. He was very tall with an immaculate oval face. He got off the bike and aimed towards her.

"My dear, why are you here all alone?"

"I lost my money."

"Go home and tell your husband"

"My husband went to court of appeal, Enugu and Anambra Judiciary staff are on strike. It is not easy for him."

"How much is the money you lost?"

"Five thousand Naira: three Thousand for antenatal and two thousand for feeding."

"Would you mind if I give you some money?"

"I have no option and I must go for antenna care. The baby is almost due."

He dipped his hand into his pocket, pulling out a two Hundred Naira bundle, removing few pieces from the money and handed the rest to her.

"Thank sir."

"You are welcome. What is your name?"

"Clara. Who are you?"

"You are my second wife. Make sure you keep that money to take care of yourself and the baby." He said, strode to his motorcycle and rode off.

Clara could not understand what the man meant that she was her second wife. She knew her husband was the only man she married and that she was the only woman in her husband's life. She kept it to herself, perusing over the the statement.

After the incident, the man kept on visiting her consoling her whenever she was moody. The most surprising moment of her life was that the same man appeared in her dream and was fighting her assailants, calling her my second wife and telling her to run for her life, that they had killed him before and could not do him any harm. When she woke her newly born baby was by the side, sleeping. Her mother in law and her mother were also there.

"Is your husband tall?" Clara asked, adjusting the pipe inside her

"Yes." Answered the mother-in-law.

"Is he fair?"

"Yes."

"Can I see his picture."

"I have it as my screensaver." She showed her the picture.

"My father-in-law calls me, 'my second wife,'" she said and told them the story.

CHAPTER FIVE
HE FIGHTS FOR YOU

He was in a cute black suit and a black pair of shoes as if he was a lawyer dressed for magistrate or customary court. On his right hand was a black portfolio containing his most valuable asset. His gait was that of a perfect gentleman. He wanted to pass a shop but had a command from the content of his briefcase.

"Chinedu, stop and enter that shop." He went straight into the porch and sat on one of the seats there. A woman, black in complexion was inside the shop. She stood up, coming out of the shop.

"Do you have coke" the man asked.

"Yes. Which one do you want _ cold or ordinary?"

"Chilled one." He said, pulling out of his pocket a white handkerchief and mopping his face. The woman entered the shop and came out with a bottle of coca cola and an opener. Chinedu held the bottle while the woman opened it.

"Chinedu, put the briefcase on the table and open it. I want to talk to the woman."

"But the woman will be afraid."

"She is even stronger than you. She has seen many tough times. She lost her parents during the Biafra war and sold edibles during the war to sustain the family. Her husband was killed by his relations? Call her."

"Madam, please do not be annoyed. Is your husband dead?" Chinedu asked.

"Yes, sir."

"Madam, don't be afraid, I go to church, even though I am a traditionalist. I worship the Almighty God but I have respect for my spiritual cock. He has a message for you." He said, opening the briefcase, a male Parrot sputtered.

"Mrs. Ikemefuna, you have a pure heart. Your husband is late but he is still around you. Do you remember what he told you about this house?"

"Yes." Mrs. Ikemefuna relived what happened. She was in a dream and her husband told him that his relations would show her where to build and that it would be on top of his grave. That as far as she would build there nothing would happen to her and the only son. In the morning the family members came to her and did as he said.

"Have you ever seen a snail at night, fall and break into pieces in your bedroom when you were living in a room and was cooking outside?"

"Yes, I remember."

"Your pot of food was uncovered when you saw the snail as pulps in the floor."

"Yes."

"That snail was sent to destroy you and your only son but your husband smashed it into pieces."

The woman was standing, both her hands folded around herself, gaping at the mysterious bird.

"Madam, please sit down." Chinedu said and took a sip of his coke.

"This is not the only case," the parrot continued, "you remember your husband's niece who had a miscarriage, losing her twins, because he went to bury a harmful charm to kill you and your child?"

"I do."

"It was your husband who neutralised and spoke to those righteous children to go out of that woman's womb. Also do you remember what a native doctor, who came to plead with you after a woman has sounded a metal gone, taunting you that soon you would be no more, told you."

"He told me that my husband warn him that if he did that charm against me and my son, he would wipe out his entire generation."

"Chinedu! Chinedu!! Those witches and wizards are still fighting the woman and the son because they don't love light, rather they love darkness and they are dark-hearted people. The bird flickered and started hovering around some areas in the compound and later landed at a place.

"This is the spot they buried the charm against your husband, yourself and your only son. It has shifted to the other place." The bed flew to the place. He landed there with his bottom feather.

"What do I do?" Chinedu asked.

"Circle it so that it can not escape the place." Chinedu obeyed and applied some substances around the circle while the parrot flew into the open briefcase.

"Bring me a shovel." Mrs. Ikemefuna went inside, came out of his shop with a shovel, and handed it over to chinedu who had worn off his suit and was wearing only a singlet and boxers. He dug the place three feet down and perspiration soaked his body as the sunlight was continuously beating him. One foot more revealed a red tied clothe, containing, a human jaw, a kobo coin, a gin drink, a perforated object, and others.

"Bring them out and bury this there." Said the parrot, picking and dropping a root therein. Chinedu covered the pit, and asked the woman for water. Mrs Ikemefuna brought a bucket of water for him. He watched and cleaned himself with a face towel, he got from the briefcase and sat down.

"He fights for you. Your husband came to me. The enemies buried these objects. The jaw is a human being that strikes one to death. It was what killed your husband. The hot drink is to make your child a drunk, the perforated object is that your son will be extravagant. He shall toil but money shall be wasted. He fights for you and he is always around you and the son. He is here. He does not want people to know about our coming; that is why we came when people have gone for schools and works. He is here and said that he is happy with you on how you are training his son. We shall leave at once, now is 1 o'clock."

"What can I thank you with."

"Don't bother. Chinedu make sure you pay for the drink."

"Please, let it be cola." She said.

"Alright, if you insist but very soon you will begin to hear news of death because they had planned to reactivate it, to take your only son. Never you tell anybody our visit, except Clara who always pays you visit. She always comes to you for the sake of your son who shall do similar work as hers. Now that you know about her, she would direct you. Anyway, once you hear about death, know that they are the people who want to wipe your family. We are leaving but I want you to know that though he is dead is still alive with the living. He fights for you." Chinedu had the parrot locked in the briefcase and left.

CHAPTER SIX

HE IS NOT DEAD

A rat flickered to and fro and hissed an agonising sound and became lifeless while she chuckled at the incident.

"What's that clara?"

"My sweet heart, you did not see what I saw?"

"I only saw a rat running as if a strange force was chasing it. But what I could not understand was how the rat could give up a ghost as if somebody hit it."

"That was what actually happened?"

"You mean somebody hit it?"

"Your late brother, Patrick, did."

"That means a soul is perished."

"Do you pity the person?"

"I do but even the Holy Bible said, 'suffer not a witch to live.' I don't understand the statement. Do you? "

"A witch is unrepentant because he does not control herself or himself. The substance in his abdomen controls him. He goes out under the influence of the object. The object becomes active once he partakes in blood, especially in the coven. Once he is given an assignment he cannot control himself until he executes the assignment. He does not know the difference between his enemies and friends, he hurts both of them. He is not tired until he succeeds in his evil mission. He can fail so many times in his evil exploration, yet, he is not tired. If you spare his life, he shall come back for you. Hardly shall he repent. He is always ready to initiate many people. This is the reason the Bible says, 'suffer not a witch to live."

"But as this mouse is killed the spirit can return to body of the witch."

"Not in all cases. It depends on the killer. If the killer possesses a power against witches, it is an express hell fire for the witch. If the killer is just an ordinary person, the witch will return to his human body. However, it is stated that if you don't want that witch to live again, once you kill any animal it has transformed into, put that animal in unused kerosene and later burn it."

"All these theories are they not superstitious beliefs. My mother told us that when they lived in Bendel state, presently Delta state, and Edo state, that was when my late brother Patrick was born, a notorious witch gave her money for the child. She collected ashes, kept the money in the plate full of the ashes, and hid it by the door side. At night, she said that she started hearing the sounds of witches but was laughing because she knew what would happen. In the morning she greeted the woman and the woman boned her. I asked my mother why the woman did not reciprocate her greeting, she said that the woman lavished those ashes instead of enjoying Patrick's blood."

"You know all these and you still don't believe." A cry thundered somewhere. The husband and wife got out of the house. A lady panted and was breathing heavily.

"What is that, Margret?"

"An old woman died but that was not the issue. Her daughters' statements are what baffle people. You can go and see for yourself." The couple moved to where the crowd was dispersing. As they were about to enter the compound, they heard, "Mama come back. Are you held where you went to? We shall fight for you?" The husband and wife were transfixed not knowing whether to go further or return. Then Clara made a u-turn and later noticed that her husband was still there.

"Vincent." Her husband got himself and followed her at once.

"Was Cecilia, that rat?" said Vincent

"Let us get home first." They said and work into their compound. As they unlocked their house, they saw a bat flying. They dunked as the bath came towards them. When Vincent wanted to take action, Clara stopped her. Some seconds after, the bath rolled on the floor.

"He is not dead. He is always here with us. He said that he must kill all those witches who have hand in his death. He was the person who hit the bat."

"Who?" Vincent asked as wailing beamed behind the compound, "Mama Joe! Mama Joe, why have you left us."

"Your late brother, Patrick, killed Cecilia and Mama Joe. He is still alive. His spirit is fighting those witches who have killed him? His annoyance is that despite killing him, they vowed that this household shall be extinct."

"Is it not better we run away from this place and go to another town and live there?"

"Their network is too much. You cannot run away from them. If you run to England, their network is there; if run to America their network is there."

"What are we going to do?"

"Get up by midnight and say your rosary. So that they cannot get up to cover your star. The rosary is a great instrument to fight them. But you must know how to say it."

"How?"

"After each decade, say your prayer point. Wage war against the forces and seal your vicinity in the blood of Jesus Christ."

"Many times, I have tried to pray but before I know it, it is morning. Even when I get up to pray, my body would be as if ten hefty men gave me a thorough beating. When I struggled despite the drowsiness, the memory of my sins would haunt me. If I continue, the next day things would begin to fall apart. I even had serious quarrel with you that threatened the unity of the marriage."

"After that what did you do?"

"I quit."

"That is where you got it all wrong. Never stop even when you feel it is hopeless to pray because your dead brother shall one day leave. He is not dead

because he is with us but one day he will leave us.
Then who will fight for you? So learn how to fight for
yourself."

CHAPTER SEVEN
CONFESS!

She could not control the impulse to light-finger the
white undies, even though she was wearing an
expensive Turkey gown, a golden Rolex watch, a
golden chain and Italian heels. A male hand caught hold
of her tightly and shouted, "Thief! thief!!" Many
marketers gathered: some in her favour and many
against her.

The detractors immediately put her in the Eve nature,
happily taking her nude pictures and posting them on
their social media. All sorts of derogatory and abusive
words condemned her. She preferred death to such a
costly embarrassment.

"Stop! Stop!! Stop!!!" Security men filed a gunshot in the air and the mundane saints withdrew from her for their life. Her rescuers took her to the White House.

"What is your name?"

"I am Mary."

"I didn't know what happened to me. For all my life. I have never stolen. Those who know me will attest to that. My husband is very rich and I am the owner of that Fetzer vehicle. It is even better if I am dead than this embarrassment. I have Five Hundred Thousand Naira in my car. The pant is very local and I have never worn such local pant before." She said sobbing.

"Say no more." Said the chairman, handing her clothes to her. She wore them and security escorted her to her car and secured her out of the market.

At home, Mary saw her property outside and her husband   at   the   gate.
"Take your property and go to your father's house. Despite all I have done for you, you went to steal ordinary   pant."
"Even you, Tony. I can't believe it. Even if the whole world can condemn me, I can't believe you will follow suit.   Please,   hear   me   out."
"I don't want to listen to your cock and bush story."

"Tony you are my childhood friend. When we were poor, I never cheated on you or steal. How then can I steal now that you are stinkingly rich? Tony, think about   it."
"I don't want to listen to the bullshit. You are a disgrace. How can I withstand the embarrassment that my wife

was naked in the market? I am now worthless. Leave here before I commit murder."

"My dear Tony, where is our love? Where are all the sweetheart, baby I love you? Never mind, I am leaving."

She drove home. The villagers, she met on her way, did not give her a warm reception, unlike before. She was convinced that the news had spread like a wildfire. As she parked into her father's compound, a woman was sitting nonchalantly, shaking her two legs. The woman did not give her an affectionate welcome as she used to, instead, she started interrogating her.

"My daughter, what is this I am hearing, that you were naked in the market for stealing a pant? I didn't bring you up in that way. Upon all the riches you have, yet you stole a pant. You have brought disgrace to this family. Your action will cause us worthlessness in this village and the church. How can I face the members of the CWO?"

"Even you, my mother," she said running into the house and coming at the rear of the house. Her thoughts were to end her life. No one seemed to understand her, except the market chairman who was not her relation. How could she face the stigma? Ending her life was what she could think of at the moment. Her eyes beheld a rope, swivel chair, and various trees, pawpaw, mango, and quaver. She took the rope and the seat to the mango tree. Mounted the seat, tied the rope to the tree and made a loop on her neck, knotted the loop strongly on her neck. She then jumped and went by the rope, her tongue rolling out.

Her spirit went to her husband's house. A lady was there. She was in her matrimonial bed with her husband.

"Cynthia, how did you know your best friend stole and was stripped naked?"

"I was in the market; I saw everything."

"Have you called her?"

"No. Nobody wants to associate with a thief, otherwise people will equally brand the person a thief "

"You were the person that sent her naked picture and told me about the incident. Why?"

"He does not deserve you. He will dent your image. I love you so much and I don't want any harm to happen to you."

"I don't know why I didn't listen to my lovely wife. I don't know why I listened to your advice." Tony said getting up from the bed while Cynthia opened her purse, smearing powder on her hand and beating her both palms together, making the particles diffuse towards Tony.

"That is by the way let us enjoy ourselves." Said Tony.

"Let us get to the market first, you promise to buy things for me." They left for the market and parked the same place Mary had parked. As they stepped out of the car, Mary appeared in front of Cynthia and disappeared. At where Mary was stripped naked, Mary appeared again.

"See Mary! see Mary!"

"Where?"

"Here." She pointing in the front

"I can't see her. Nobody is where you are pointing."

"She is there."

"Confess!" Said Mary running around her like a lightning.

"I shall confess. I made Mary steal the pant. I am aware that when a woman steals in the market, she must be stripped naked. I made you see her action and consequences as unforgivable. I want to have you as my lover." Tony's phone rang, and he looked at it. It was Mary's mother. "Your wife is dead. She committed suicide."

"Oh my lovely wife." Said Tony, collapsing. After the incident Tony's character changed. His wife photo was always his companion. Most times, he brought it out, tears twinkling down his face as he lamented, "how foolish was I not to have listened to you. I shall not have any sexual relationship with any woman again in my life. Please, forgive me." Each time he was sobbing, Mary was with him trying to console him and tell him that he had forgiven him but he was spiritual blind. However, Mary sought the assistance of Clara who convinced Tony that Mary had forgiven him and he should get married again.

CHAPTER EIGHT
I AM YOUR SON

She saw an elderly man coming towards her. Her mind told her that the man was not ordinary. She crossed the road to avoid interacting with him. Raising her eyes, she beheld the man, already in her front

"Please, grant me audience. I want to speak with you." He caught her attention.

"Good morning sir, what can I do for you?"

"Good Morning, Clara. I shall never forget what you have done for me?"

"Where? I have never met you before? I don't even know you? Anyway what have I done for you?"

"Do you remember what happened to you sometime 2008 at Awka road, Inland town, Onitsha?"

"I do and I can never forget the incident." Clara's mind reviewed the event. She was feeling hot and had a terrible kick inside. What her body wanted at the moment was something chilly. Her mind suggested Five Star at Awka road, Onitsha and her body obeyed. She purchased a can of ice cream and was trekking down passing Tasia, ABS junction, Mba road. In front of General Hospital, a red corolla vehicle hit her and she fell into a lorry, full of sand.

She touched herself, thinking she was in the spirit world, and felt severe pain in her abdomen. People brought her down from the lorry and suggested taking her to the hospital but she asked for her bag. Her phone was still intact. She placed a call and in ten minutes an ash camry car packed by the side and a man sauntered.

The man examined her there and told her that the child was intact but the baby was still eight months and her stomach was opened. She asked the man to take her to his hospital and never to let her husband know about the accident. The doctor accepted, took her to the hospital and treated her.

Her husband complained of a rotten smell but she attributed the odor to her pomade. Whenever she took drinks, some would go out of her stomach. Once her husband was around, she always covered the body and quench the taste of taking drinks in his presence. The doctor warned her of her life but she was afraid her husband would for the sake of her life, forgo the child

"I am your son. I am your son, Patrick, you suffered for. Not every woman can do what you did for me" He said, cutting short her recall. A passerby stared at him wonderingly and he returned the stare ferociously whereas the woman averted her eyes, increasing her pace.

"What exactly do you want me to do for you?"

"Sorry my dear, don't mind the busy body. I want you to take care of me."

"How?"

"My mind is in one of your sons. He is the most intelligent of all your children but doesn't know how to read. He lacked the foundation because negative forces were and are against him. I was given the privilege to come back to this world through him to correct all the atrocities committed in the past but have my limitations. When you had the accident, I fought for your life but when Patrick was born, I was not given the opportunity. You and your husband should fight for me. I want you to know one thing: God cannot do for man what man can do for himself."

"Please, my dear. I am fainting, I have not taken my breakfast. What do you want me to do for you?" He gently placed his two palms on her shoulder.

"It seems a surge of energy envelopes me."

'Alright. Your son, Patrick, some negative forces are still fighting your son Patrick. A teacher in nursery three, used chewing-gum to collect Patrick's hair and used it against him. Also in Primary three, a lady gave a knock on Patrick's head, intensifying the charm. Patrick suffered severe headaches for three days and after that his comprehensive ability became retrogressive. Instead of praying for me, you and my grandson started calling me dunce. I am not blockhead; Patrick is not dunce. I cannot save myself but you. It was your son's cries that made the God almighty, after my series of appeal, to send me to you."

"What then are we going to do?"

"Make sure you don't use words of curse on your children; rather, words of blessings. Make sure that your family take bath before going to sleep: water has a neutralizing power. Occasionally, break coconuts and let the family take the water and watch your heads with the water pronouncing words of blessings and neutralizing all evil pronouncement."

"Thank you so much but what can we do for Patrick?"

"Parents have power over their children. Let my grandson and my father, your husband, break coconut and pronounce words of favour over Patrick, canceling any evil pronouncement on Patrick. Let him also map out time to teach Patrick. At first it will be difficult but let him have patience with Patrick. Patrick shall learn. I am your son and blessing to you. If you take care of me, Patrick, you not regret it but shall be happy ever after. Remain blessed." He said and left.

CHAPTER NINE
THE MIRROR OF THE PAST

He lay on a bed gasping for air. He had been taken to so many hospitals in different parts of the world but his money could do nothing. He wondered what futile life, he had lived for his unbridled quest for money. Regrettably, the said money could not save his life. He wondered whether God could forgive him. For the sake of money, he had sold his soul to devil, but could he redeem it at the last minute. No repentance in the grave whirled in his mind.

Could he set the hands of the clock back, he thought but no one could do that. How foolish he was, he shook his head and remembered the past.

He had a lovely family: a beautiful wife who begat three daughters and a boy for him. They lived as a happy family, except that they were not financially stable. Service of God was their priority. All his efforts to make it financially seemed futile, despite his faithfulness in worshipping God. He thought the best option was to dine with the devil.

His first assignment as a member of a secret cult was to sacrifice his most precious jewel, the pride of a married African man: his only son. The second sacrifice was the only person that had ever satisfied him in bed – his lovely wife. Others were his last and second daughter. Only one person survived the sacrifice and that was her first daughter who had married before he joined the society.

"Clara," he called as a lady stepped in with a girl, "I'm dying."

"Your impatience and lack of faith were the cause of your problem."

"How?" He said, fighting hard to breathe.

"Mother, Ambrose, Lucy and Jacinta always visit and complain that it was your foolishness that destroyed our lovely family. I would not have been here if not for your granddaughter, Mary who insisted we should come to see you" Clara waited for him to respond but he did not. Mary removed her scapular and placed it on his neck.

Clara and Mary watched the spirit leave the body. It was as if heaven opened and they saw a big head looking like a shadow, surrounded by seven archangels, Michael, Gabriel, Raphael, Uriel, Barachiel, Sealtiel, and Jehudiel. Blessed Virgin Mary stood at a side while a fragile old man, his body emitting splendor on the right side of the black image and the third person of the Trinity stood on the left.

"Charles is mine." A very pretty being beamed.

"Lucifer, look at Charles' neck."

"He has a scapular on his neck but he killed Martha, his wife, Ambrose, his only son, Lucy and Jacinta, his daughters."

"He is saved by grace. Her daughter Mary saved her?"

"He has sold his soul to me."

"Heaven and earth shall pass away but every bit of my words shall come to fulfilment. Mirror of the past" Lucifer disappeared. Two cherubs, brought the mirror of the past while others were enchanting.

"Hossana in the highest. Hossana in the highest."

"Charles suffering and time of blessing." The cherubs instructed the mirror as the Above ordered. Charles appeared in the mirror, worshipping God with the family members. Most times he was in anguish, thinking that his prayers and efforts were unanswered. The mirror showed Archangel Barachiel with host of angels showering blessings upon blessings upon Charles who had joined secret society, sacrificing members of his family, thinking that the society blessed him.

"You were created to live Hundred years but they made you live fifty years." Said the above

"So this useless society made me destroy my lovely home."

Clara wept as the vision disappeared.

CHAPTER TEN
HE MUST MARRY ME

His voice was persuasive, captivating, and enchanting, especially among women. Nature endowed him with a beautiful appearance: he was fair, slim fit, and had an oval face with a pointed nose. Most women adored him for any time spent with him was lovely. Any woman he went to bed with would never leave him,

He changed women as clothes and women fought among themselves, trying to have him solely. Ladies flocked to him and patronized him with gifts but only one woman whose sensual beauty he could not resist, even though he did not know her genealogy, was hard for him to woo.

“What is your name?”

“Ann.”

“Magnus, I have warned you to stop pestering me.”

“You are the apple of my life.”

“I don’t think you need the apple. You have so many women in your life.”

“I have decided to settle down with you.”

“What you want is my under. Once, I give it to you, you will dump me.”

“I shall never do that to my love, my nectar. Whenever I see you I find it difficult to control myself.”

“You are even unable to control your libido, as it is clear from the protruded object under your legs in your trousers.”

“My sweetheart, I am dying for you. I can do anything for you”

“Swear, you must marry me and shall live with me for eternity.”

“I swear.”

“It is sealed. Tonight I shall come to your house to take you to mine”

"Do you know my house?"

"Which lady in this town does not know the house of the minister of women's affairs?"

At night Ann came to Magnus's house and both of them, hands entangled, strolled to Ann's house.

"This road leads to MaryAnn's house."

"Who is Maryann?"

"A lady that wanted to hang someone's pregnancy upon me." She disengaged her hands from his, as she let a bunch of keys fall to the ground. With the light of the moon, she saw the key and stooped. Her body was fuming in annoyance. She waited for a little on the ground to steady her shaking hands.

"But you abandoned her?" She said in a hushed voice and got up.

"No, I didn't. I told her that the child is not mine. The next thing I heard is that he committed suicide."

"Because you cared not!" Her voice exhibited an annoyance that sent a shiver to him.

"My sweetheart, do you know her? You are taking it personally."

"So this how you are going to leave me?"

"God forbid."

"So be it?"

"When did they build this beautiful house near the market, I thought I walked past here the day before yesterday. That sight was the location where Maryann was buried." He wanted to voice it out but held himself so as not to exasperate him more.

"This is where I live all alone."

"This house is very beautiful." She unlocked the house and they entered. He saw a fascinating wardrobe, undressed, and hung her clothes. Two of them started swimming in the ocean of love.

Throughout the night, he was inside her. In the morning she started experiencing penis captivus. Many people gathered around, watching him as he was lying naked on a grave and his clothes hung on a newbouldier calmbodies. He was struggling to get up but could not. To his sight, his genital organ was glued to hers but observers saw him naked, lying flat on the grave, pushing up and down.

"Abomination. Magnus! Magnus!! This is not ordinary. He was responsible for the pregnancy." He couldn't hear as people where saying all sorts of things. His body was full of perspiration.

"Maryann." Clara who just arrived and understood the incident said, "have mercy on him, you have thought him a big lesson. For the rest of his life he can't do it again."

"He must marry me. I love him so much."

CHAPTER ELEVEN
WARN THEM

He took her from one room to another, showing her all his hidden treasures. After which he led her into the parlor and sat down on a goatskin mat on an arm seat, pointing at the sofa for her to sit. She sat and her eyes focused on her regalia. It was an immaculate white, glittering. Her stare caught sight of a golden chain on his neck and a sparkling white pair of shoes on his feet.

"Clara, you are a woman of integrity, and people revere you in this our town. I have great respect for you. I know you will deliver my message. Take a look at the mirror." He said, getting up, strolling at the back of the seat, and stopping by the sink. Clara's eye took a glance at the mirror but reverted towards the man who had unlocked the tap and was watching his hands.

"Ojinnaka, I can't see anything in the mirror."

"Clara, please, look in the mirror." Her eyes focused on the mirror and the image of a man appeared in the mirror.

"I know him, sir, but I don't know his name."

"His name is Lawrence. I brought him up. His gratitude to me is to sow seed of discord in my family. You know what is happening in my family."

"I do, sir." Clara answered reliving the incident. After the death and burial of Ojinnaka, the family received a letter for the unsealing and reading of Ojinnaka's will. The family honoured the invitation and the will bequeathed all the property to the second wife, Gladys and her only son, Cyprian, except where the first wife, Cordelia was occupying which according to the will should revert to Cyprian, Ojinnaka's only issue, after the demise of Cordelia.

Cordelia lamented that her husband could not make such a will and that Ojinnaka and her acquired most of the properties together. He later sued Gladys, Cyprian and probate Registrar. The matter was pending at court 2, Awka. As a plaintiff, Cordelia started first and fielded two witnesses and tendered so many documents to prove that Ojinnaka did not make a will. She later closed her case and the defendants opened their case, fielding two witnesses, remaining their last witness, Lawrence.

"Tell Lawrence," Ojinnaka said, "to remedy what he has done. I shall disgrace him. Tell Gladys and Cyprian that I am not happy with them and they should take a new leaf. Tell my wife to be calm that I shall never allow her suffer. Warn those evil people. Warn them. Warn them." Clara woke up and a cock crew. She looked at the wall clock: it was 6:00am.

Her husband Vincent had already woken up and was preparing to court. She told him about her dreams. He told her that he would be in the same court. She told him he would follow him to the court but would first of all deliver the message. Clara took her bath fast and went to Ojinnaka's house.

She met Lawrence who was dressing up. She told him the dream but Lawrence paid deaf ears to the warning. She also met Gladys and Cyprian who equally did not heed to the warning. When she delivered the message to Cordelia, Cordelia was filled with joy. She then returned home and went to the court with her husband.

At the court, Ojinnaka approached Clara. "Thank you so much for delivering my message. I have permission from the Above. Watch and see what will happen." Ojinnaka went and sat in the witness box. Nobody was seeing him except Clara.

"Court!!!" A Clark of the court beamed when a knock emanated from inside the judge's chambers. A tall, black-complexioned man sauntered and everybody stood up.

"Good morning everybody. Mention your cases." Lawyers mentioned their cases in accordance with the seniority at the bar, determined by the year when they were called to the Nigerian bar. Ojinnaka blew air towards the judge.

"Please, the most senior lawyer, I shall do number 5 first in the cause list which is number 13 in my list. Clark of the court please call number 5 in the cause list."

The suit number A / 210 / 2008 and the parties were called. They answered their names and came out to stand by the dock.

"Appearances." Said the judge.

"With humility, my lord. I am A. C. Obi, I appear for the plaintiff."

"May my lord be pleased. C. C. Okeke. My representation is for the defendant."

"No representation for the 3rd defendant, the nominal party," the judge asked.

"My lord, 3rd defendant is represented by P. C. Ifeoma and she is aware of today's proceedings. Besides, she did not file any pleadings in this case." Said Barrister A. C. Obi.

"What is the position?"

"Evidence of Dw3, our last witness."

"call the witness."

"Lawrence." The defendant counsel called, as Lawrence walked into the witnessbox. Ojinnaka entered into him and clara chuckled in smile.

"Tell the court your name?"

"My name is lawrence Okolo"

"What do you do for a living."

"I am a teacher."

"Where do you live?"

"I live at No. 150 Oguta Road, Onitsha."

"You made a written deposition in this case on 22nd day of June, 2010."

"Yes."

"You want to adopt the said written deposition."

"No." There were hiss and boos in the court and the defendant counsel was embarrased. "I want to state here that it was not Ojinnaka Ambrose Okolo who made the will. I, Lawrence with Gladys and Cyprian made the will. We made the will and lodged it when late Ojinnaka Ambrose Okolo was sick in the hospital."

"Lawrence, do you know the implication of what you are saying." Asked the judge.

"Yes, my lord. We committed a criminal offence, forgery."

"You know you can be prosecuted for that?"

"Yes, I know but I want to clear my conscience. I am having a prick of conscience."

"My lord, that's all for the witness." Defendants' counsel said dejectedly and sat down. He later stood and said, "My lord can I seek the leave of this honourable court to cross-examine him as an adverse witness."

"Counsel, you are free. This is your witness."

"You were paid by the plaintiff to come and give this false information."

"I am not. I was even the person that briefed you and not the other defendants. I masterminded the whole will."

'My lord, that is all for the witness."

"Plaintiff's counsel, do you have any cross-examination." Said the judge

"None, my lord since the witness has confessed that he made the will."

"My lord, the defence closes his case. I shall need thirty days for my address."

"Plaintiff's counsel, how many days do you need?"

"My lord, thirty days."

"Defendants' counsel, you have Seven days for reply on point of law if any. Is 6th day of October, convenient for both of you" The judge asked.

"Yes my lord.' Answered both counsel. The court started writing and later read out.

"The case is adjourned to 6th day of October, 2010 for adoption of written addresses, thirty days to both counsel and seven days to the Defendants' counsel for reply on points of law." As court pleases. Ojinnaka left Lawrence and Clara laughed hysterically, going out of the court.

"My lord, I have not given any evidence." Said lawrence while the clark of the court asked him to step down from the witnessbox and people started laughing in the court.

"Silence." The Clark of the court ordered as the orderly of the court moved his physiques, sending a signal of arresting anybody flouting the order of silence. Plaintiff's counsel did not look at him but left him as he was still in the witness box when another matter was called. He then left the witness box, wondering what happened.

"Warn them! Warn them! This is just the beginning." Ojinnaka told Clara who went to Gladys, Cyprian, Barrister Okeke who were blaming Lawrence and told them that Ojinnaka Ambrose Okolo was still warning and would do more harm if they did not repent.

CHAPTER TWELVE
MY BELOVED

Goosebumps were all over his body when he woke up, stretched his right hand for his bedmate but no one was there. He sighed, wanting to cover himself with the bedsheet on the bed, but decided otherwise when he caught the sight of his window. It was open. Opening his mosquito net, he came out of the bed and aimed at the window. He closed it and went inside the room where his son, daughter, and sister-in-law were sleeping. The room was freezing as if the AC was on. A cooling breeze emanated from the windows, he rushed and had the windows locked.

He heard a buzzing sound. It emanated from his bed, under his pillow. Raising his pillow, he saw his phone. He picked it up and noticed it was 3:0am. He knelt down to pray and tears trickled down his cheeks. Nevertheless, he managed to say divine mercy prayers.

After the prayers, he retired to bed but was unable to sleep. Memories of his sorrow were all over him. He tried hard to suppress them but to no avail.

The 22nd day of December 2002 was the day he would never forget in his life. It was raining that day. He was the person that went for the school runs while his lovely wife was at home waiting for him. His wife was doing her master's at Enugu State University of Science and Technology (ESUT). As he returned from school runs, he took his wife to Peace park, Oguta Road Onitsha.

"Tony, I'm having cold feet about this travel." She said as she was about entering a bus.

"Lizzy, but you shall miss the exam if you fail to go" He kissed her on the cheeks and bade her goodbye. She entered and the bus took off.

Around 6:00pm, he called her phone but she didn't pick. She continued calling but no picking. At 6:30pm, he called and a male voice answered, "Hello."

"please, give the phone to my sweetheart."

"She is in the casualty ward, University Teaching Hospital Enugu."

"What is she doing in UNTH, Enugu?"

"He was knocked down around Holy Ghost Catholic Church."

"Can't she talk?" He asked, entering his vehicle and driving off.

"No!"

"Who are you?"

"Dr. Sylvester."

"Please, Dr., take good care of her. I am on my way to Enugu. I am coming from Onitsha."

"We are doing our best." The phone went off. It took him an hour and thirty minutes to reach UNTH, Enugu. He called the doctor on the phone who directed him to his wife. She was lying motionless on the bed with a drip on her.

"My sweetheart, my beloved. Lizzy" Her mouth was closed. He touched her and felt her breathing pulse. Throughout the night, he stayed with her until at 3:00 am after saying his divine mercy, Lizzy started having hiccups.

"Take good care of our children and marry my beloved"

A flash of lightning flickered through the window and he was jolted to reality. He picked up his phone. It was 3:40 am. He came out of bed and went into his children's room where the lightning wafted, but could see nothing. Since her wife had gone to the underworld, he had been having this lightning experience but couldn't understand. He vowed to unravel the mystery surrounding the lightning and who her wife meant by my beloved.

The next day, he traveled to his wife's town and met his parents-in-law and a lady discussing.

"In-law, you shall live a long live. We wanted to come to your house later. What Clara is telling us is strange."

"What is that, Clara?"

"Your beloved is here besides you and she wants you to marry her beloved."

"Who is her beloved and the lightning that traverses the house?"

"Your wife said that she is the lightning."

"But who is her beloved? Her last statement in the hospital is take good care of our children and marry my beloved? Is her beloved the eldest sister, Stella?"

"She said that Stella is self-centered and cannot take good care of his children and you, her beloved."

"Who then is the beloved, I shall marry."

"The youngest sister, Cynthia "

"How can. That means commission of abduction. Cynthia is seventeen years old and a minor."

"She said, 'she is the only person that can make you and the children happy. Next year, she shall be eighteen years. Marry my beloved, make her happy and I am happy"

"I shall marry Cynthia, she has been living with us and I understand her character"

"She is very happy and bides us goodbye."

"Thanks." They said as Clara left.

CHAPTER THIRTEEN

COURT SESSION

Vincent was sitting among his learned colleagues when he heard the blaring of siren. Looking back, his eyes caught the sight of a white vehicle pulling to a stop at the entrance, where canopy of lawyers was at the left and that of the DJ, staff of the court, visitors was at the right.

"Court!!! The administrative judge is coming out to receive the corpse of professor Joshua Ikenna Okonkwo" A lady registrar beamed as everybody stood up. Vincent's eyes cast towards the front, beholding a canopy, inside it was a table well designed with white clothes. At the left was a canopy and the occupants were all senior advocates and the state attorney general. Beside it was a lectern and another canopy giving shield to the lady registrar who was holding a microphone. At the right were two canopies, one for the bereaved and the other for the magistrates, presidents and members customary courts. Behind her was a canopy where judges were and the administrative judge with another judge stepped out, passing the registrar, senior advocates, the vacant table, walking down the steps and aimed towards the vehicle which back was open, showing the casket containing the professor.

A lawyer was already by the side, holding a microphone. As the judges drew nigh, he said, "As the chairman of this noble bar, I hereby hand over the corpse of Professor Joshua Ikenna Okonkwo to the Administrative judge of the high court."

"I, justice Chukwudi Okonkwo, hereby admit the corpse of professor Joshua Ikenna Okonkwo into the court." The judges returned and some lawyers carried the coffin and deposited it on the vacant table.

"My lords," said the registrar," the corpse of Professor Joshua Ikenna Okonkwo is in the court, we call on the attorney general of the state to present an address in memory of Professor Joshua Ikenna Okonkwo.

Five lawyers in procession, proceeded towards the casket, bowed for the legal luminary therein. Four of them climbing the steps, grouping themselves into two, each group franking the corpse at each side and the five simultaneously bowing at the corpse. The lone lawyer returned.

A tall fair man in wig and gown stood up, he read an address in memory of Professor Ikenna Okonkwo and submitted the address to the registrar.

"My lord the address of the attorney general is hereby tendered." Said the registrar.

"The address of the attorney general is admitted in evidence and marked as exhibit A." Said the Administrative judge.

"As the court pleases," answered people.

"We call on the most senior advocate to address the court in memory of Professor Joshua Ikenna Okonkwo." Said the registrar.

The same counsel appeared in company of another four lawyers, repeated the process but returned with the original companions.

A short black man stepped outside and went to the lectern. He read a tribute in the memory of the professor and handed it over to the registrar.

"My lord, the address presented by Julius Obiora San is hereby tendered."

"The address presented by the learned silk is hereby admitted in evidence and marked as exhibit B" said the admin judge.

"As the court pleases."

"We call on the chairman of the bar to present a tribute in honour of the professor."

Also, in company of another four legal practitioners, the same lawyer appeared, repeated the process, substituted the old with the new and returned with the old.

The NBA chairman presented a tribute in honour of the deceased and later handed the address to the registrar.

"My lord," said the registrar,' the address of the NBA chairman is hereby tendered."

"The address of the NBA chairman is admitted in evidence as exhibit C." said the admin judge.

"As the court pleases." Replied the people while the registrar said, "we now call on the administrative judge to give his judgment about professor Joshua Ikenna Okonkwo."

Justice Chukwudi Okonkwo, coughed, clearing his throat and started speaking,

"My lords spiritual and temporal, my learned brothers, the honourable attorney general, the learned silks, the magistrates, the registrars, presidents and members of the customary courts, members of the outer bar, ladies and gentlemen, all protocols duly observed.

Today, we are all gathered here for a virtuous man, professor Joshua Ikenna Okonkwo, who announced his appearance in the court as J. I. Okonkwo. Professor J. I. Okonkwo esquire lived a very good life. He is my uncle and my mentor in the legal profession. If not for him I would not have been a lawyer, let alone a judge..."

Vincent phone vibrated continuously and he could not concentrate on the administrative judge speech. He looked at the phone. It was fifteen missed calls and the caller was his sweetheart. Also he saw a message, "Darling, where are you?"

"In the front." he replied.

"Let us go."

"Why?"

"I am not comfortable here and they are here disturbing me. They are happy I can see them."

"Who?" He texted and her and saw two men opening the casket while judges started filling past and bowing for the corpse.

"Dead lawyers, judges - they all came for court session and are happy I can see them"

"Where are you?"

"Under the fruit tree but they are making me look insane."

"Ignore them. Once I take the bow, we shall leave." Later lawyers queued up, marched towards the corpse and bowed for him one after the other. Vincent joined the queue, bowed and walked towards the fruit tree.

"Clara, are you going. Thank you so much for coming to my court session." Said professor Joshua Ikenna Okonkwo as Clara and Vincent left the scene.

CHAPTER FOURTEEN

MY ONLY SON

A man walked to and fro shouting, "my only son." Nobody listened to him. All his efforts to catch people's attention proved abortive. Tears trickled down his cheeks.

"What happened to your only son?" Asked a woman, at the sight of the tears.

"Did you see me?"

"What do you mean?"

"I died last year in a ghastly motor accident."

"Clara, you and the dead people." She walked past him

"I'm sorry, please by 12 noon tomorrow, my son shall be dead. Please call my brother, rev. Fr. Anthony to pray and save my son."

Clara stopped but the sight of two women, one fair and the other, black, caught her attention. Cyriacus knelt by her side as she watched the women in the verbal combat.

"I have warned you severally to remove your items from that space but you refused. Whether you like it or not you must remove it." Said the black lady.

"You cannot do anything. This is my space. I paid for that and my shop." The fair lady replied, adjusting her goods towards the space.

"I only pity your son, Cyriacus. If not the love I had for the father, I know what I would have done to you." Hearing his name, Cyriacus ran out of the shop and embraced her mother from behind.

"My leg, my leg." Cyriacus released her and stared at her mother who was rigoring in pains and afraid at the sight of her sudden swollen leg. Surprised at the occurrence, Cyriacus rose, approached the young Cyriacus and the mother but was unable to express his empathy.

"Rita, my sweet heart." Cyriacus wanted to touch her but could not.

"You have done your worst. Do you have the interest of Cyriacus at heart, yet you have the heart to poison the mother." Said Clara.

"I didn't do anything." Answered the black lady.

"Did I call your name?"

"But you were referring to me."

"Is anybody selling white chalk, nzu?"

"Mama Titi, the Yoruba woman," answered Rita

"What can I do for you?" Asked Mama Titi who appeared from her shop.

"Do you have Nzu?" Clara asked.

"What is this?" Shouted MamaTiti looking at Rita's right leg. She later brought white chalk and gave it to Clara.

"Who knows what she has done that made her a widow and now she is infected with Enyiule."

"Shut up Blessing. Your name is Blessing but you are a curse." Said Mama Titi.

"I have done nothing against her."

"We shall know very soon. Rita, may I help you out." She said sitting down and raising her legs. At the centre of her palm, she drew a circle and with her right hand held the place tightly and tugged it. Forthwith, ten formidable centipedes gushed out of the palm.

"Jesus!" Observers shouted.

"Back to the sender." Said Clara robbing an olive oil on Rita's palm.

"Fire! Fire on my leg!" Blessing recoiled in pains and became afraid as she saw her right leg continuously swelling up.

"Why did you do it? Why do you want Cyriacus to be an orphan?"

"I didn't do anything. I love Cyriacus."

"Alright, I shall leave. Do you know the rules governing this charm?"

"It is more poisonous to the sender. Please forgive me. It is hatred. I love her husband, Cyriacus. I thought Cyriacus would have married me but he married her. After the marriage, Cyriacus died and my hatred toppled against her. It is because of the love I had for her husband that I am very fond of her child Cyriacus who is a replica of his father. I loved his father but Rita was a misfortune. Whenever I see her, I see her as the cause of the death of my Cyriacus. If Rita dies, I shall take the responsibility of bringing up Cyriacus for the sake of my Cyriacus."

"How did you get to know about the spiritual poison?"

"Somebody did it to me in this line and I decided to use it against another."

"If you know that you're the one, you had better confess before it would be too late." Clara said while eyes cast from place to place to know the culprit.

"I'm leaving."said a man in a knight regalia.

"Charles, my husband, relax: it is not yet time for the meeting. Have you forgotten we are going together. Wait let us know the evil ones in the line. Firsthand information is the best information." A fair lady said

"Okay, Lizzy" Said Charles sitting while his heart started palpitating.

"I'm warning for the last time. If you are the one, come out." Clara said and pulled out those centipede from Blessing. They maneuvered on the ground, sending shivers down the spine of some of their viewers.

"Please, the person should come out." Said Lizzy.

"Back to the original sender."

"I'm dying! I'm dying!!" Shouted Sir Charles.

"What is that, my sweet heart?"

"My leg, my leg."

"Jesus! So I have been living with an evil man."

"I'm sorry my sweet heart, I belong to a secret society. I used those centipedes against my enemies. I used it against her because she wanted to investigate the death of my brother, Cyriacus. With that I diverted Blessing's attention from diving into the cause of the death of Cyriacus."

"So you killed your younger brother. I thought you loved him so much."

"I did and that was what led to his death. The society took him from me as my beloved. Sad enough the society is trying to take his only son, Cyriacus, by 12noon tomorrow. I also killed our only daughter Margret"

"You are callous, Charles and deserve to die," said Lizzy.

" Now that the Centipedes are inside you, prepare for your death? Call your brother, Fr Tony to give sacrament of confession. Do you want to die?"

"I don't want to die."

"What is the rule of the poison?"

"The society told me that once the centipedes get into my system, there is no remedy."

"So you will die?"

"I don't want to die"

"You love to take ice cream and pizza?"

"Yes, I do."

"Madam, go to ShopRite and get pizza and a bucket of ice cream for him because by 12am tomorrow, he shall die. If he dies without taking them, his spirit shall be roaming, hunger for pizza and ice cream but shall never get them."

"I shall do that for him. Can I go now?" Lizzy asked.

"No, call fr. Tony so that he shall confess his sins. His soul will go to purgatory instead of hell fire." Said Clara while Lizzy took her phone and dialed the number.

"Please, I know, I don't deserve to live but have mercy upon me." Said sir Charles.

"Hello, Fr., I'm Clara. Where are you?"

"In my parish, St John the Baptist, Onitsha."

"Your brother, Charles is dying in his shop at Oze market and needs the last sacrament."

"I shall be there immediately." Said Fr. Tony who later came in five minutes. Tony was surprised when he heard the story. Sir Charles confessed his sins while Tony gave him penance and absolved him.

"Clara, is there nothing we can do to safe both young Cyriacus and Sir Charles."

"We have to do vigil because the cult shall operate at night to take syriacus and when they can't get you Syriacus, they would fight sir Charles." Clara said, healed sir Charles and left

However, the family and Clara held night vigil at St John the Baptist's chapel. At 12.00am, the fraternity struck both their prayer destroyed the Society. Cyriacus was happy that his only son was safe. He bade them goodbye. Clara notified the family who waved back.

CHAPTER FIFTEEN

DESTINED TO BE GREAT

A man drove to St Michael hospital and took his wife and his newly born child in his vehicle and drove outside the hospital. On the road, the man noticed that he was being trailed. He could see nobody on the road that he diverted to, only bushes on the left and the right with the chirpings of birds and the cracklings of insects.

His eyes caught sight of a pathway. He stopped the car alighted, kissed his wife and his son, "hurry, take the route and walked straight, I believe, it is safer."

"Sweet heart, what about you?"

"Start going before they catch us." He entered the vehicle as he heard the footsteps of his wife towards the pathway. The footsteps became faint and he saw the flash of the car. He looked towards the pathway when the car light flashed but did not see his wife and son but only shrubs and slight pathway in between the shrubs. He was convinced his wife and son were saved.

He sped off and his trailers followed suit. He was happy that his wife and son were safe from those people. A feeling that wide reptiles might attack them sent shiver over him. He continued speeding, his pursuers were still pursuing him.

He drove inside the bush, stopped the ignition, jumped out and ran into the bush. His trailers stopped and one of them fired a gun. Both of them jumped out of their car, slamming the doors and running towards the car. They flashed their torches.

"Odogwu, nobody was in the car." Said the one that fired the gun.

"Hitman, they are not far from here." Said Odogwu, flashing his torch light everywhere.

"That's Williams, shoot." Sounds of gunshots wafted via the direction Williams was running to. Williams diverted to a pathway and a flash of bullet shot past him as he fell down and got up again, his heart palpitating fast. He continued running until a bullet got him at the back, piercing the left front of his heart. He dropped down. The men rushed there and shut him severally, making sure he was lifeless.

"Where are the child and the mother?" Asked Hitman while Odogwu was flashing the torch light everywhere but no sign of human being but incessant sound of crickets and some animals. They searched and searched until they were convinced the mother and child was not there. They then left

Williams spirit rushed to the vicinity where his wife and son was and noticed that his wife was at the verge of death in a pull of blood while a cobra encircle his son, protecting him against any adversary.

"look for Clara. She knows what to do." Said the child. Now the spirit of the woman met her husband and they left. Soon they returned with Clara who was in a cloak.

"I have finished my work." Said the python, disengaging from the child.

"Thanks." Said Clara and the child.

"I shall take the child to the person who will bring him up. The enemies will think all of you are dead. He is destined to be great and his name shall be Patrick." Said Clara disappearing in cloak with Patrick.

CHAPTER SIXTEEN

THE INCORRUPTIBLE VIRGINS

Clara strolled along Ridge road, Onitsha. She saw two ladies indecently dressed standing in front of Nibbles gate. The rays of sunlight was piercing gently.

"What big fishes the harlots are trying to cash this morning." She thought.

"We are not harlots, stop seeing us as such." The one in Patra nicker and sleeveless blouse snapped.

"Who are you? What then are you doing here in this early morning, dressed like this?" she asked, sliding her palms, pointing at them.

"I am Ifeoma and she is Nkiru. We are waiting for our killer." Said the one in short sleeveless gown, looking lascivious.

"Your killer! How?"

"We were kidnapped and killed ten years ago by a man." Said Nkiru.

"For ten years, you are still following a man, why?" Asked Clara.

"He kidnapped, killed and cast us into a lagoon somewhere in Lagos." said Ifeoma.

"Somebody told us that the person who would help us would come and we are waiting for the person." Said Nkiru.

"Our family doesn't even know that we are dead and we want the man to confess." Ifeoma said.

"Alright, I wish you people good luck. Continue waiting for the man." Clara said crossing the road. She saw a mad man sleeping comfortably at the back of Onitsha court at Ridge road. She passed the man and was heading to EEDC office (popularly known as NEPA, when a lady appeared before her.

"Clara, my friend, please help them." She said.

"Olivia, for long I have not seen you?"

"Your tears are too much for me to bear."

"I regret that I couldn't resuscitate you?"

"It's not your fault and you really tried to prevent the ugly incident."

"I did but all my efforts were fruitless. I have never been so annoyed as I was then. Whenever, I see you, I remember the sorrowful event" Clara said reliving the past.

Alexander was making advances towards Olivia but Olivia was not interested. Whenever Alexander saw Olivia, Clara and Philomena, he would lurk at a hidden place, admiring her after he had received a serious warning from Clara not to disturb Olivia. He found it difficult to control his libido at the sight of Olivia. One day Olivia was on a lonely place when Alexander pounced on her and deflowered her. Clara gave Alexander thorough beating that led to his admission in the hospital.

After some months, Olivia missed her period and realized she was pregnant. Clara notified Olivia's parents who promised to keep the pregnancy. Unfortunately, Olivia's mother later started disturbing Olivia to commit abortion but Olivia refused.

On one fateful day, Clara and Philomena came to Olivia' house so that they would go for a football practice. The mother told them that Olivia was not around. The mother had injected an abortive substance into the juice he gave to Olivia. Olivia fell asleep and later started having profuse bleeding and was taken to the general hospital Onitsha. As fate would have it Olivia gave up a ghost and her body was deposited into the mortuary before Clara and Philomena came. Clara wept and always lived with the regret, that he could not revive her friend.

"Clara," said Olivia cutting into her reverie, "what are you thinking? Look back."

As Clara looked back, she saw the two ladies on their kneels, showing their opened palms and the back, as a sign of plea for Clara to come back.

"I told them you are their solution. Please help them out."

"You know I need the permission from the Above before I can help them out." The rays become intense and Clara cast her eyes up and saw the approval in the sky. Clara crossed the road to meet the duo.

"Please, help us out our bodies are still intact. We want the man to confess so that our parents would know we are dead and bury us." Said Ifeoma.

"How can I get the man; I don't have his phone number."

"leave it for me." Said Olivia leaving the place in a fluke and coming back in a speed of light.

"Have you got the number?" asked Clara bringing out her phone from her blue jean trousers pocket.

"Yes," Olivia replied, giving it to her.

Clara added the number and put a call across.

"Hello, who are you?"

"Clara, I'm at the gate waiting for you."

"I don't remember having appointment with any lady."

"Come out, I am waiting for you." Clara said cutting the phone. A minute after, a fair handsome man came out.

"Are you Clara?"

"I am."

"You are epitome of beauty."

"Thank you." Clara focused on her neck. He wore a golden Rolex necklace.

"I believe you are hot in the bed."

"What is your name?,"

"Douglass." He said, trying to steal a kiss from Clara who held him by the neck, lifting him up and placing him on the wall by the gate. She ordered him to be speechless or she would kill him. She waved into the air and to his consternation saw three female.

"Ifeoma and Nkiru are dead. I killed them so many years ago."

"You are going to confess and show the family where you dumped their bodies."

"Their bodies can never be found. They have decayed. I threw them in a lagoon in Lagos."

"Our bodies are still fresh." Said Nkiru.

"If your bodies are still fresh, Clara can revive you." Said Olivia.

"Is it possible?" Asked Nkiru.

"It is possible. We shall leave Douglas alone, otherwise people shall become afraid of you."

"Douglass shall not go scot-free. Even Lucifer cannot commit such an offence." Said Ifeoma while Douglas knelt down pleading for forgiveness.

"I swear today to live a good life. A man called Akataka gave me the assignment to kidnap them. I kidnapped them but Akataka killed them and asked me to dispose their bodies into the Ikeja Lagoon which I did. "

Clara used her cloak and took them to Ikeja in Lagos state where Douglas pointed the spot and Clara resuscitated Ifeoma and Nkiru who were happy. Akataka confessed and died while Douglas later became a pastor.

CHAPTER SEVENTEEN

YOU CAN SIN EVEN IN DEATH

Clara sat on a rubber seat and her attention was on her friend who went to call a person. A lady wanted to sit on a seat beside her.

"Someone is on that seat but you can sit here." Said clara looking at the vacant seat but surprisingly saw a man trying to sit there.

"When she comes, I shall leave." Replied the lady.

"You know her?" Asked Clara.

"Who?"

"Philomena."

"She is my childhood friend. We lost contact when he entered secondary school."

"She is also my friend. I know her in the secondary school and we are in a football team. I came to this burial because she asked me to accompany her. According to her the burial rite is for her primary school childhood friend, Chisom. I believe you should know the person?"

"I am the person."

"What do you mean?"

"My body is lying there. Take a look at the poster you shall notice, I am the one. Do you see that fat woman in CWO uniform, over there? She was the person who killed me. She came to the burial to cage me and to kill my brother"

"What is her name?"

"Madam Cecilia."

"She is a witch." Said the man.

"I know, I can perceive her scent. Who are you?"

"I am Chike. Look at me very well. Didn't you hear of what happened at Isiokwe road where a woman confessed killing me and died thereafter. I met a native doctor who helped me out. With the assistance of the medicine man, I was able to take my revenge."

"So both of you are dead. Are you not aware that you would be roaming the world until the number of the years the Almighty destined that you would leave the earth?"

"We are aware."

"Are you aware that you can sin even in death."

"We are not."

"You should be careful because whatever sin you commit here, even though you are dead you will still be judged. It is better to plead with the Almighty God to grant you permission to do the revenge, than doing the revenge yourself without permission from the Above."

"I don't want to know. This woman killed me and she must die." Said Chisom, fuming, causing cyclic wind while people started shouting that the dead people were going to the market.

"Reduce your anger. You even possessed some powers which you don't know. Pray that the Almighty God shall send you back to remedy the wrong."

Philomena walked to the scene in company of a man.

"Coach Sam, good morning." Said Clara.

"Good morning, Clara. How are you?"

"Fine."

"Clara, are you going to mass or are you staying behind?"

"I shall go home."

"Please, don't go." Said Chisom

"Chisom, I shall go. You don't want to listen to me."

"She wants to kill my only brother, Uchenna."

"She cannot, I promise you. I got approval from the Above to be here. I don't normally go to burial, especially when the person is lying in state. I shall help you out. You have to excuse me, I have a work to do" Said Clara while Chisom and Chinedu left.

"I was carried away. I was talking to your friend, Chisom"

"Chisom! Chisom!! Where is she?"

"Lower your voice. She has left but wants a revenge.'

"I miss her."

"Madam Cecilia killed her "

"Madam Cecilia is a CWO president and goes to morning mass everyday."

"Are you doubting me again?"

"Sorry, my prophetess."

"Coach Sam, I shall leave. We shall see later."

"Alright, my dear." Said coach Sam

"See you next time." Said Philomena.

"Bye" said Clara leaving.

CHAPTER EIGHTEEN

THE POWER OF ROSARY

He always said his rosary everyday, before going for morning mass or Sunday mass. In his prayers, he remembered all his family members: his wife, children and siblings. Also he prayed for the repose of his parents. Most times when he mentioned the names of his parents thus, "may the souls of Mr. Paschal Okonkwo, Mrs. Regina Okonkwo and all the faithful departed," his parents were with him but he couldn't see them

On 20th day of August, 2006, he had a persistent Knocking on his doors when he was saying his prayers. His family members travelled and he was alone in the compound and wondered who was knocking. Opening his gate, he came face to face with a lady.

"Who are you and what are you doing in my house this early morning"

"I am Clara. I have an urgent message for you. Are you not Mr. Anthony Okonkwo?"

"I am. What is the message?"

"Your parents are happy with you for putting them in your rosary. Your rosary has served as an indulgence for them, aiding them gained access from purgatory to heaven. Also, because of your rosary we are here to save the life of your younger brother, Ignatius who is in danger. Your parents were given the grace to talk to me and save Ignatius."

"I saw Ignatius yesterday. He is hale and hearty and will be in the church."

"We have no time left and if your brother dies, his blood, shall be upon you. Let us go to the forest"

"To the forest, forest, no! First of all we go to the church and his house."

At the church, mass was going but Ignatius was not there. Anthony went to the sacristy.

"Did you see our catechist."

"He hasn't come. I wonder whether he is well. Catechist, I know comes here everyday before anybody. It's unlike him." A boy in red cape, white surplice, red gown and white canvas, answered.

Tony and Clara left for Ignatius house. At the Ignatius house they knocked severally and later a woman in a wrapper and a rumpled blouse came out

"Good morning, where is your husband?"

"I don't know. He was wearing a short nicker and a singlet with a rope in his hands when he left the house"

"Did you ask him where he was going?"

"No, I didn't.

"Are you not aware that he supposed to be in the church?"

"'Yes, I am"

"You saw him dressed like that and you didn't stop him?"

"Ignatius is an adult and can take care of himself?"

"Which route did he take."

"The path leading to the forest."

"And you never care to stop him!"

"Ignatius is old enough to feign for himself."

"If anything happens to my brother, I shall hold you responsible.' Anthony strode towards the forest while Clara followed suit.

"No, take your left." Shouted Clara as Mr. Paschal Okonkwo directed her when Anthony got to the junction having two paths.

"Lord, I have served you for several years yet I am childless. My wife is high blood pressure to me. I am no longer happy. I am ending my life. Please lord forgive me and receive my soul…" They heard and saw him naked, knotting the rope.

"Ignatius! Ignatius!!" The rope fell and his brother held him and later picked up his clothes. Clara stood by the side while Anthony approached him.

"My brother, I am tired of this world."

"Please, wear your cloth, first."

"Naked I came into the world, naked I want to go to my creator."

"Please, let us go to your house?"

"My wife is a devil incarnate, I'm sorry to say that. I cannot go back to my house. He calls me impotent, poor church rat and all forms of derogatory words, yet she is a Charistimatic. When people see her sing and pray in the church, they think she is an angel."

"Please wear your nicker first and let us go home. Our kindred shall deal with her " He wore his nicker and hung his singlet on his shoulder.

They returned to Ignatius house and Chinelo heaved a heavy sigh, muttering some incoherent words

"If I don't know you well, I shall call you a witch" said Clara staring at Chinelo who clenched her hands, menacingly approaching Clara and stopped. Clara laughed and remembered how she beat two young men that were disturbing Chinelo.

"Have you brought the Tigress." Chinelo said.

"Nobody is here to fight you, if not for our intervention, you would have been a widow."

"Is it not better that he is dead, so that I will be free."

"Stop that clamp." Anthony's face turned red, his teeth gritted, his fingers tightened but he held his emotions.

"Please sir, calm down. The lord has heard your prayers. Let our lord, solve the problem."

"Chi, Chim, please, sit down " Chinelo's face radiated and she sat at the extreme while her husband was at the other extreme of the couch. Ignatius wanted to get up but remained still when he saw that her wife was not sitting close to him.

"I don't want to lose my only brother. Is it not better the marriage is dissolved. Fr Anthony is working in the Secretariat and can help us out."

"It has not gotten to that. Chinelo is a nice woman to live with?"

"Not true. She is a heart attack!"Ignatius snapped.

"Also our catechism is a lovely man to live with?"

"How I which you were not married. I would have given him to you." Said Chinelo.

"Your parents go to 5:30 mass, I want them to be present."

"knock, knock." Said the same boy who was at the sacristy when Anthony and Clara came to the church.

"Enter!" said Chinelo.

"Good morning."

"Good morning, Obinna, what is the problem."

"Fr Anthony sent me to come and check on the catechist."

"You know Mr. and Mrs Okafor, the parents of catechist's wife." Asked Clara.

"Yes ma, I know them. They are in the church."

"Tell them and fr. Anthony, that we need their presence in Catechist's house."

"Alright," said Obinna, leaving.

"Your marriage is threatened, you need the power of rosary. Catholics don't know what they have. Anyway, before I delve into rosary, I shall want you to bare your grievances. Whatever that is your annoyance against each other, I want you to voice them out. Please, when one is speaking, the other shall not interfere. Catechist, please start first."

"No, let her start first." Said the catechist.

"I married my husband as a virgin. When we started we did two or three rounds everyday but later my husband started starving me of sex. Every moment he was in the church. Whenever he was around, he would tell me he is tired. Even when he gives me time, he only satisfies his urge, leaving me to suffer. I hardly reach my orgasm whenever I am together with him. Most times, as I walk along the road, I feel sexual urge to commit adultery. Besides, the money, he is giving me, is not enough for the family. I have told him to open a business for me and he said he doesn't have money. Inside me, most times, as I look at him, I am filled with strange anger. At that instant, I condemn him with words and start destroying our belongings. After sometime, I feel regret but could not explain the feeling."

"Ignatius, is that what happened?"

"Yes. He always disturbs me with sex, I virtually don't have property at home because of her violent character. Most times, I keep late and stay back in the church because I hardly have peace of mind in my home"

"Greetings" said Mr. Okafor coming in with her wife.

"Mr. and Mrs. Okafor we thank God, your in-law is not dead?"

"What happened?" Mrs Okafor asked.

"You shall later know. Only tell us the truth."

"Which truth?"

"You are an Ogbanje, Am I correct?"

"Ogbanje, Ogbanje."

"Tell us the truth."

"I am."

"You have a husband and children in the marine world? Is that correct?"

"It is correct?" Mr. Okafor turned and stared at her wife

"Peace be unto this house"

"Welcome, fr. Tony." They said together.

"Clara, the great woman."

"Sorry father, don't feel annoyed that we invited you here. I hope you don't have another mass?"

"No, I don't."

"Your catechist nearly commit suicide. But that is not the issue now. I hope you are still saying the rosary at 12 0' clock?"

"At first, it wasn't easy for me. Any time, I wanted to say it, one thing or the other will distract me. With conscious effort, I have succeeded and I don't miss it, except when I am celebrating the mass."

"Mass is the first in the spiritual ranking and rosary is the second."

"You know yourselves but there are two persons staying with us here, Mr. Paschal Okonkwo and Mrs. Regina Okonkwo. You don't see them but I hear and talk to them."

"They are dead?" said Fr. Anthony.

"You have the power to see the spirits, the angels and to perform lots of miracles but you have to say your rosary at 12:00 am every night to develop yourself. You remember what happened in your parish and why you started saying your rosary at night."

"I do." Replied Fr. Anthony reliving the incident. It was in 10:30am mass on Sunday. A tall black huge man, about fifty six years old with a fair beautiful lady about fifty years old were in front of a procession. The man was carrying a baby girl while the woman was carrying a baby boy. Eight of the people coming after them had eight ropes, raised up while a lady carrying a big brown envelope was directly at the man's back. Songs of offertory were in pace but the couples and his companions, except Clara, were mute. Everybody was dancing in jubilation.

Rev. Fr. Anthony was surprised as he saw eight ropes. He took the female child while the man looked back and the lady gave him the brown envelope. After saying words of blessing the father handed over the child to the Lady originally with the brown envelop and then collected the boy, repeating the same process and handling him over to the mother. The man handed the black envelop to rev. Fr. Tony, saying, "Vour hundredi thousand nira dey for de envelop for the cows."

They knelt down, Fr Anthony blessed them, sprinkled water on them and took a microphone, saying, "Please, can someone tell me what is happening in this church because from the attire of this people they are Muslims."

Clara stepped forward, taking the microphone from rev. Fr. Tony. "In deed they were staunch Muslims but now Christians. Mrs. Fatima Haruna saw me in the grotto of the blessed virgin Mary, saying my rosary and asked me whether that woman answers prayer. I answered in the affirmation and she asked me to teach her which I did. I also told her she could say it any time but the best time is twelve midnight and twelve noon that blessed virgin Mary normally appears at the time. She started visiting the grotto, saying her rosary at twelve noon and at home, twelve midnight."

"Our lord is great, our lord is great. Catholics don't know what they have. Blessed virgin Mary, as you all know visited three children, Lucy, Jacinta and Francisco, in 1917 during first world war, which started in 1914 and promised that with rosary the war would come to an end which happened in 1918. Also she told Lucy that Russia must be converted if rosary would be said daily."

"But father, you are not praying daily as at when do and our lady wants you to be doing that. Many times, she has appeared in your dream."

"That is true. I hereby promise never shall a day pass without my saying the rosary."

"Father Anthony, Father Anthony, what are you thinking?" Asked Clara jotting him out of the reverie.

"It was a memorable day: I shall never forget that day. I thank God for using you."

"God wants to use you in a great way and your power is rosary. You had an accident and you thought it was the work of the occult people that came for burial where you had the accident. No, it was Ifeyinwa, your cook who is also the daughter of Mrs. Angela Okafor"

"I don't have any daughter by such name." said Mr. Okafor.

"I know."

"Ifeyinwa is not even from this town and he is not related to Angelina Okafor." Said Fr. Anthony..

"Ifeyinwa and Chinelo are twin sisters and the children of Angelina in the marine world. Mrs. Angelina and Ifeyinwa are aware of their powers but Chinelo is not aware. It is the operations of her peers in the Marine world that make Chinelo most times weird. Mrs. Angelina Okafor, are you not their mother in the spiritual world."

She wanted to lie but the splendor emitting from Clara's eye compelled her to answer in the affirmative.

"Chinelo can never beget any issue for Ignatius and she doesn't know about that."

"Ifeyinwa came to work in the father's house to kill limit your powers. Many times she has tried to seduce you to crush the gift in you. She always applies some charms in your food to make you prayer ineffective and your spiritual powers, inactive. She was the person that caused the accident to blind your spiritual eyes and not that cultist you thought."

"I shall strangle her for causing me a lot of harms."

"It is not the battle of the fresh but the battle of the spirit. Remove anger from yourself because soon they would attack for their secret is revealed. Now let everyone be in the spirit of prayer "

A minute after Ifeyinwa emerged, her eyes dark red and her mouth muttering some incantations. Clara's eyes turned red and a pythons of light shut out of her palms, engulfing Ifeyinwa and her invisible companions. They all vanished except Ifeyinwa who fell down exhausted and unconscious. Clara then performed exorcism on the Chinelo, Ignatius and Angelina

"Say your rosary everyday." She told them and left with Mr. and Mrs. Okonkwo while rev. Fr. Anthony was dumbfounded.

CHAPTER NINETEEN

THE ANCESTORS

Clara's eyes beheld two young men ringing a bell as a handsome fair man with three other men, in chieftaincy regalia and some men in ozo attires and some others in ordinary wears, approached majestically. The four men in chieftaincy wears were all stamping their spears as they marched in synchronization of the music, they were enchanting.

At a time, the fair man dashed out like a lightening, danced and danced. "Onowu, the prime minister, the king maker, the greatest dancer." Said his followers.

"Darling, are you hearing any music?" Asked Clara.

"No!" Answered barrister Vincent.

"Ezennia, do you hear any music?"

"No." replied Ezennia.

"Are you people, not seeing anybody?"

"We are only three here – you, your husband and myself."

"They are spiritually blind and deaf. Tell Ezennia that we, the ancestors are here. He should not be afraid, he is fighting a just course and we the ancestors are solidly behind him. Let him remember to call us before he goes to court. We are here to assist him. That man shall never be a leader over them. How then can he summon us since he doesn't have blood relationship with us. Besides, he is a curse to the family because his father is not happy with him. Allowing him to be a leader over them means incurring the curse of the father in our descendants. Look at the father, very embittered." Said Onowu pointing at a man standing by.

"I am Mr. Kingsley Uzoma. I cohabitated with Madam Rose and begat barrister Nnamdi. I christened him Hyacinth when he had his baptism. I was there present with the mother Rose when he was baptized. I personally, because I loved him dearly, took him and brought him back throughout his primary school. He answered my name from infant, primary and secondary school and later changed his name in the university because he wanted to be famous. He was the reason I am in the underworld."

However, Clara relayed the message to Ezennia who performed some spiritual rites in the morning, convening the ancestors who came, although he was not seeing them. After that Ezennia proceeded to court. The judgment was given against barrister Hyacinth Nnamdi Uzoma but in the favour of Ezennia and the kindred.

As barrister Hyacinth Nnamdi Uzoma stepped out of the court, he fell, trying to get up, he fell again. People gathered around. Ugochukwu, who gave evidence for him during the hearing of the suit, offered him a seat, aided him to wear off his shirt and started fanning him. Ezennia and his family members chuckled and stated that the ancestors were dealing with him.

Clara who witnessed the incident, understood what happened. Mr. Kingsley Uzoma was enraged with the attitude of his son and was the person that made him fall and was still raging that he would do more if his son would fail to do the right thing.

The victors went home happily. Gunshots sounded into the air as merriments prevailed in the family. As the living were dancing, the ancestors were in a festive mood also.

CHAPTER TWENTY

THE DEED

She saw her parents, who left her home over an hour ago, come back.

"What is the problem? Did you forget anything?"

"Cynthia, we forgot to give you a deed," said the father.

"Which deed?"

"Deed in respect of the land I purchased in G.R.A. Onitsha.

" Where is the deed?"

"It is in the car and the car is open. Get down and take it?"

"But you just came out of the car." She walked passed them, came to the door, and saw the door locked. Her thought was that she was the person that locked the door and had not opened it. She wondered whether she forgot to lock the door when her parents left. She suppressed the thought, got a bunch of keys from the center table, unlocked the door and got downstairs.

The look of the car was different from the state it was when he saw them off one hour ago. She entered the car and her eyes searched all the places and captioned three documents, each of them was headed, the deed of assignment. She picked them and went back to her house.

"You know the house I bought at GRA, Onitsha, I showed you."

"Yes, I do."

"Is now yours."

"But Daddy, you told me that you purchased it One Hundred and Fifty Million Naira and that you would relocate from Awka to Onitsha to live there."

"I said so but I am changing my mind. I shall no longer need it."

"Yes, we no longer need it." The mother concurred.

"My daughter, make sure you don't give the document to anybody. Don't give to your uncle, your mother and even myself. The house is now yours. Go there now, the rooms are open. Don't waste time in locking the place. Once we leave here, go and lock the place. In life, I want you to learn one thing, no matter the circumstances you see yourself, always be happy and glorify God"

"We shall miss you."

"I don't understand, I thought you bought the house to be close to me. Besides, the house is very big, it can contain both families."

"Don't bother my daughter. We love you so much. You are a blessing to our family. We are happy to have you as our daughter." They left.

Her phone rang after five minutes that her parents left her house. She picked it. "Are you Cynthia, the only daughter of Mr. Innocent and Rita Ugwunta?"

"I am," answered Cynthia.

"Your parents had a motor accident one hour around Ukpo at Enugu Onitsha express road and they are dead."

"It is not true, they left here five minutes ago."

Cynthia notified her husband about the incident. They went and locked the house at G.R.A. Onitsha before, going to Ukpo. They took the corpses to the mortuary. Cynthia's parents were buried the same day. After the burial, her uncle demanded for the deed but Cynthia kept her father's instructions. Her Uncle then instituted an action in the court.

Two judges who tried the case died at the eve of the day of judgement. There was fear among judges that judges were dying in the same court. The third judge before seating in the court invited Clara.

"I know, I have some spiritual powers but I need your assistance to know what is killing those judges. These are all the case files in this court. Check them and the court room to know if there is any negative things there. I don't want to die. I love my wife so much and I am enjoying this world. I don't want to die. You know that my parents wanted me to be a priest but I told them I can never leave my honey and I can never imprison my manhood. My sweet heart, am I not saying the truth."

"Yes, my honey, you are on the right track." Said the wife.

"Justice Jude and barrister Evelyn Obiajulu. you will never kill me!"

"We love being together. We shall live long, die and be buried together."

"Wait." Said Clara when she touched a file. The whole problem is in this file."

"Bring it aside. What is the actual problem?"

"Look around and tell me whom you see. You have the power, use it"

Justice Jude Obiajulu waved his right palm in the air, trying to catch something and his sight caught Innocent and Rita Ugwunta.

"I know you very well when did you start using cloak."

"They are dead." Said Clara

"Why are you here?"

"We need justice."

"How?"

"I didn't give my brother, my house. I gave my only daughter the deed. Those judges died because they took bribe and wanted to give judgment to my brother."

"I am an incorruptible judge and can never stoop so low to collect a bribe. You are even my Godfather. My father is Nicholas Obiajulu."

"Jude, my son. You know that I and your father are very good pal. I am happy to see you. I don't have to bother again. I gave my only daughter the deed in respect of the property at GRA Onitsha and no other person. We shall leave, do justice." The deceased couple vanished and Clara later left.

Justice Jude Obiajulu gave the case accelerated hearing. Later Mr Ugwunta, after the adoption of written addresses, came to bribe the judge who rebuked him.

Besides, Mrs Ugwunta had told her husband to withdraw the frivolous suit but he refused. She reminded him the good things his late brother did for them and that the conception of the children they had was possible because of Cynthia. She had the memory of the incident.

Mrs Ugwunta had had several miscarriages. One day she and the husband visited Cynthia's parents. They were in the parlour discussing when Cynthia, a girl of three years then ran to her with a cup of water.

"Anty, take this water. It is good for your health." Everybody was surprised and the woman drank the water. Cynthia touched her stomach, mumbling something and later said, "You shall bear a boy and a girl." She took the cup and left. Ten months later the woman gave birth to wonderful children – a boy and a girl as Cynthia prophesied.

On the day of judgment, Mrs Ugwunta was in the court and judgment was given in favour of Cynthia. Mrs. Ugwunta embraced Cynthia and congratulated her. Mrs. Ugwunta got home packed her belongings and left her husband's house, telling him that she could no longer live under the same roof with a wicked man.

ABOUT THE AUTHOR

Patrick Chidi Anyaegbuna is a lawyer, writer and motivational speaker.

HIS BOOKS:

A. FICTION

1. THE BARBARIC DOGS THE BARBARIC DOGS

2. THE HURRICANE THE HURRICANE LINK

3. EVEN GOD

4. ASUNDER

5. THE HEALER

6. THE DEAD ARE ALIVE

7. THE REJECTED STONE

B. NON FICTION

    1. MASTER YOUR DESTINY

- His Website books' link